Tales from the Coffee Shop

Annette Francis

Tales from the Coffee Shop
First published in Wales in 2003
on behalf of the author
by
Bridge Books
61 Park Avenue
Wrexham
LL12 7AW

A CIP catalogue entry for this book is
available from the British Library

ISBN 1-84494003-9

Printed and bound by
Ashford Colour Press
Hampshire

For my Father
ARTHUR FRANCIS VIDLER
5 February 1926 – 28 February 2000
With love and treasured memories.
I wish he was here to be proud of me.

Contents

Introduction

I was born in 1958 in Wrexham and have lived most of my life in this area. After attending Yale Sixth Form College I gained employment with a well-known bank where I worked for 22 years. Due to illness I left my job and did not work for two years during which time I dabbled in an ambition I had harboured since my teens — writing.

I had a some success, but many setbacks. When I was fully fit, I managed to acquire a waitressing job. I could not face returning to banking and needed something completely different.

The summer at 'The Plassey Leisure Park' is lively and busy and I have no time for any other work, but in the winter months when it is quieter, time allows me to pursue my ambition.

The collection of short stories in my book are based on truth and many situations described have actually happened. Working in 'The Stables Coffee Shop' has changed my life, for the better I might add, and I hope you enjoy reading my book as much as I have enjoyed writing it.

Annette Francis, 2003

Autumn

Broken Hearts and Teacups

"Round, round, baby, round, round," Annette sang abysmally, but she was quite partial to the Sugababes latest hit. She turned the volume up even louder on the car radio then indicated to turn right into the 'Plassey Leisure Park' where she had been working for the past year. It was a long, winding drive, regimentally lined with beech trees and bronze lamps, towering from old-fashioned posts. Sheep were grazing on the one side whilst the Friesians, opposite, were forming a queue along the hedgerow, searching for the last remnants of foliage to munch and chew. It was the prettiest morning she had witnessed so far. The October sky was the clearest azure and the low, autumnal sun dazzled her lovely, hazel eyes forcing her to draw down the visor clipped above the windscreen.

She parked around the back as usual, gathered up her full-length black skirt and clambered awkwardly out of the car. The crisp, fresh air slowly wafted up her nostrils and she felt enormously exhilarated. She glanced up, instinctively, as the tower clock struck nine and caught sight of someone standing in the turret window.

"Strange." She thought. "I've never seen anyone up there before." But there was no time to ponder.

Today was the first day of the Edwardian weekend, celebrating one hundred years since the estate had been established. Originally a farm, the cow shed was now an exquisite restaurant, the stables a cosy coffee shop and the rest of the site had been transformed into small craft units which still retained their 'olde-worlde' charm with original red-brick buildings and latched barn doors with milk churns standing guard.

With a distinct spring in her step, Annette walked vigorously towards the Visitor Centre, a sort of mini museum detailing the history of the complex. She darted down the narrow passage, in too much of a hurry to digest any of the information littering the walls, and reappeared in the early sunshine. Her auburn twirls of hair bounced and glinted beneath her homemade doyley-style hat and her Edwardian apron of brilliant white cotton, broderie anglaise lace and satin ribbon, was blinding in the vibrant daylight. She waved to Auntie Mary in the ice-cream parlour and bounded into the coffee shop kitchen. Her boss was there already.

"Morning Carlton."

"Good morning, Annette."

He turned to face her.

She spluttered and almost choked.

His lips weren't visible at all, only a thick, black, hairy moustache twizzled neatly at both ends. He had pasted it conspicuously under his broad nose and the bowler hat, perched on his jet black hair, reminded her of Hercule Poirot.

For a moment or two they were in hysterics and Carlton's 'Scooby-Doo' laughter echoed around the white-washed walls.

"I ... bet ... Joanne was in stitches ... this morning." Annette chuckled.

"She was still asleep. Thank heavens!"

A tall, striking man in his late twenties, Carlton was a generous, agreeable proprietor. His deep, dark eyes held a mischievous twinkle which attracted a variety of ladies to frequent his establishment on a regular basis.

On his days off, Annette was often asked,

"Is Carlton in?"

Pleasantly, she would repeat her standard reply. "No, I'm afraid he's not today."

Under her breath she would, boringly, whisper to Sheila, the third member of their culinary team,

"If I had a pound ..."

Finally regaining control of themselves, the Edwardian duo set about their daily tasks. There was fresh salad to prepare, coffee to brew, cutlery to polish and menus to arrange. An hour vanished into oblivion and, needing a breather from the cucumber she was slicing, Annette dreamily stared through the kitchen window. She absorbed the sheer beauty of the Welsh hills in the distance and reminded herself how lucky she was to have landed this job. At long last she felt at peace with herself. The last three years had been particularly tough. She had endured a heart-breaking divorce, the traumatic death of her father, major surgery and had renounced a high-powered executive career. At forty, she had thought her life was over, but then had met and married her adorable Julian. He had made her feel special, helped her regain her shattered confidence and encouraged her to accept the work on offer. Julian and Carlton had, unwittingly, given her a second chance and now she knew the true meaning of being 'blissfully happy'. Her pensive thoughts were sharply interrupted. Sheila had also been greeted by the, less than subtle, black moustache and was in tucks. Clutching her sides, she looked absolutely stunning. Her Edwardian waitress attire suited her slender, petite figure perfectly and accentuated her flawlessly tanned skin to the utmost. Her short, brunette hair and make-up were immaculate and, today, she had an air of mystery about her which was incredibly appealing. In the short time the two women had worked together they had become good friends. In fact, the three of them had gelled into a well-organized and professional team. They trusted each other implicitly and all possessed a finely-tuned sense of humour, bouncing harmonious banter like ping-pong balls. The atmosphere was always bright and breezy inside, whatever the weather outside, and their customers never failed to receive a friendly, hospitable welcome. In fact, great pains were taken to cheer up any down mouths and, with this in mind, Carlton occasionally dared them to make even the most despondent of his clientele smile.

"Annette", he would ruse, "I'll give you a pound if you can make the woman on Table Three even half smile."

Always one to take on a challenge, she would cajole and chat to the chosen misery and most of the time was successful, but Carlton would refute her claims,

"Oh no, no, no! You don't get your pound that easily. She had wind!"

By opening time, everything was in its rightful place, the front door was unlocked and the customers flooded in. Coffees, teas, teacakes were briskly served up and by lunch time they were snowed under. Hot meals were dished out with absolute precision and numerous wedges of delicious cake, oozing with cream and decorated with a sprinkling of icing sugar, were cut meticulously. Despite being rushed completely off their feet, they endeavoured to maintain their exceptional service.

"Lasagne and a curry for Table Two! ... Tuna pasta bake, ham sandwich and soup for Table Five!" Carlton yelled out the finished orders as the two waitresses scurried and scampered, this way then that, distributing the meals with energy and enthusiasm.

"Carlton! I need a poppadom." Sheila implored in her low, husky voice.

"I want a bread roll," Annette was fraught, "... and, by the way, I hope that's cheese dangling from your moustache."

By two o'clock, they were on adrenaline. Orders abundant, afternoon teas a-plenty and coins clinking every few minutes as they were thrust into the tips tray.

Suddenly, a resounding cheer went up in the courtyard and the hustle and bustle was briefly disturbed. Unable to contain her curiosity, Annette felt compelled to investigate. A beige coloured horse-drawn carriage was pulling up. There was a crest on the side, but she could not quite make it out over the heads of the crowd. The coach door was opened by a fake footman and His Worship the Mayor planted his foot vigilantly on the first step, his gold chain draping forward as he lowered his head. She peered around at the familiar faces of the shopkeepers she knew so well, but there was one face there she could not recognise. The unfamiliar woman, staring straight at her, had entered into the spirit of the occasion wearing a very good imitation costume. She squinted, hoping the face would become clearer, but, for a split second, she was distracted. Someone was placing their arm through hers, huddling up beside her.

"Isn't this wonderful?" Auntie Mary's left eye always twitched when she was excited.

Annette was about to ask her aunt who the unknown woman was, but, by the time she had returned her tentative gaze, the woman had disappeared without trace. "Funny?", she thought, but then her attention was again side-tracked. She had caught sight of a seemingly never ending column of bicycles, weaving and gliding their way up the drive. Dry days, even in winter, brought out the cycle clubs, but today of all days. She dashed back into the coffee shop to warn her unsuspecting colleagues of the impending invasion. Two by two the skinny, tight lycra legs clumped through the door, fluorescent yellow helmets were removed and the exhausted pedal pushers plonked themselves down.

Battling her way to Table Four, Annette flipped open her order pad, poised for action.

"Beans on toast, white bread, no butter."

"Two rounds of brown, buttered toast with beans on the side."

"White toast with butter, beans on top."

She was amazed at how many ways there were to consume beans on toast. She fixed her eyes on the ninth member of the group, waiting in anticipation of yet another method of serving up, what was fast becoming, the 'delicacy of the day'.

"Beans on toast followed by fruit cake with a cherry on top and I'll settle up with you in the men's toilet."

She glared coolly into his confident, green eyes. Unperturbed, she floored him with one swooping sentence.

"There's only ONE fruit cake in this coffee shop!"

Reduced to fits of laughter, the rowdy rabble teased.

"Aye, you've met your match there, Tecwyn … Not often you're speechless … and he's blushing."

Tecwyn went very quiet and tolerated the taunting and torment doled out by his fellow cyclists.

Meanwhile, Annette had retreated to the kitchen and placed the scribbled order on the rack. Carlton emptied numerous tins of baked beans into a massive saucepan and switched the cooker ring to full power.

There was a sharp knock at the back door.

"I'll go." Annette unlocked the top half of the stable door and came face to face with the woman she was unsure of in the crowd.

The woman's features were young, but her complexion was a pale grey which made it difficult to determine her age. She wore an elegant, royal blue crinoline dress, edged with delicate white lace. A matching bonnet with silk ribbons hid most of her hair, but Annette observed a stray blonde curl which had escaped onto her forehead.

'Why don't I recognise her?' She was puzzled. 'I thought only the traders were wearing Edwardian costumes, but whoever she is, she's done a brilliant job. It looks very authentic.'

"Is my husband in there?" The woman asked in a faint, troubled voice.

"Possibly." Annette felt decidedly uneasy."What's his name?"

"William."

Not wanting to linger any longer than she had to, "I'll ask for you."

She wandered around the tables,"Is there a William in here? ... William? ... No William?" No-one owned up.

Her search was disrupted by a loud crash from the vicinity of the open-plan kitchen and everyone clapped and cheered. Why customers partook of this ritual whenever one of them dropped crockery, was beyond her comprehension.

She found Sheila sweeping up the remnants of two broken teacups which had been scattered in every direction imaginable.

"Sheila! What have you done?" Annette winked at Carlton revealing a cheeky dimple.

"It wasn't me, they just fell off the drainer."

Annette slunk, apprehensively, to the back door, but the mysterious woman had again disappeared.

"Weird." She muttered."Where did she go?" She quizzed her companions.

"What woman?" Carlton wasn't particularly interested.

"Oh, never mind. What's that smell? CARLTON! THE BEANS!"

Black didn't even come into it. The beans had been cremated and were at one with the pan.

"I can't believe you've burnt the beans, baked beans of all things, after all the wonderful meals you've churned out today!"

Sheila was trying very hard not to show her amusement and Carlton tutted very loudly, biting the rim of his moustache so he would not swear in front of the ladies.

Late afternoon was looming and murky clouds were congregating over the hills. Rolling mist began to creep, languidly, across the fields. It would not be long before the next nasty weather front reared its ugly head. Fortunately, most of the day's activities had ended. Only the 'Milk-a-Cow' competition and the coconut shy were still doing business. People slowly began to make tracks and the weary workforce started the big clear up.

Annette treated the floor to a bucket of hot water and plenty of Flash. She loved the way the wet tiles gleamed, swishing the mop to and fro. This was her last task each day and it gave her immense satisfaction. Many thought she was nuts. When all the chores were over and done with, they relaxed with coffee on Table Five. Sheila left first, grabbing her coat, and Annette was not far behind, bidding farewell to an exhausted Carlton who was left to lock up. It was drizzling quite hard and the dark, heavy clouds were lurking ominously as Annette headed for the Visitor Centre. All the lanterns had been lit but, instead of tearing straight through, blinkered, as she normally did, she paused and glimpsed around.

The walls were hidden by glass cabinets containing all manner of curiosities. There were chambermaid outfits, old farm implements, pieces of jewellery and antique furniture all dating from the turn of the century. Her attention was, inexplicably, drawn to the photographs displayed in the smallest of the cabinets. Her eyes widened as she recognised the woman on the first picture standing next to a handsome gent. She read the description underneath and held her breath, shocked.

Charlotte and William Brookshaw. Founders of the farm and estate in 1902. Shortly after, William went missing on the day of the annual Autumn Fair, 19th October 1902. His wife died of a broken heart six months later when she discovered he had, in fact, emigrated abroad with a young girl from the local village.

An icy chill raced through her body. It was the date which really hit home, spooking her into a cold sweat. Today was the 19th October 2002, exactly one hundred years to the day William Brookshaw had absconded. Shivering, she sensed something behind her and froze, unable to move. She could not even swallow the colossal lump in her throat. It touched her shoulder and her mouth gaped, but she could utter no sound. A simple squeal would have sufficed, but nothing.

"What's wrong with you? You look as if you've seen a ghost."

Annette spun round and, for the second time in one day, caught an eyeful of black, hairy moustache.

"Y ... y ... you ... idiot!" she stammered."You scared me to death!"

She was visibly shaken and Carlton became concerned.

"What on earth's the matter?"

"That's her!" Annette gestured at the photograph.

"That's who?"

"The woman who came to the back door at lunch time."

Carlton peered at the picture and read the narrative.

"It can't be her, she died almost a hundred years ago."

"I know, but I swear, Carlton, that was her!"

One of the lanterns flickered and a bitter gust of wind whistled its way through the dim passage. Fallen leaves and debris, sucked in by the current, rustled and swirled around them. They glimpsed at each other, momentarily, and Carlton gulped. Without any more ado, they hared towards the exit and, somehow, both managed to squeeze through the narrow entrance, popping like a champagne cork into the rapidly brewing storm.

They halted, breathless, sure they were safe in the confines of the car park and leaned against Carlton's BMW. Giggling nervously, they hid their trepidation, but both were feeling pretty stupid. Eventually, they calmed down, soaked through to the skin.

"You'll be all right going home?" Carlton was very protective of his staff.

"Yes, thanks. I'll see you tomorrow." Annette was shaking, but she kept it under control. She climbed into her own car and started the engine. Carlton waited until she had pulled away before revving up and following her.

As both cars glided down the sloping driveway, they were unaware of their audience. The silhouette of an Edwardian lady, standing in the clock tower window, sadly watched their departure. A solitary tear trickled down her cheek and dripped on the sill, just as the heavens opened.

Ooh! La! La!

It was Annette's first day back at work after a glorious sun-filled fortnight in the Canaries. She slowed at the top of the Plassey's drive and, between the strokes of the windscreen wipers, could see a naked female mannequin, nonchalantly, leaning against the brick wall. She parked the car in the usual spot and giggled to herself towards the coffee shop.

"Morning, you two! Glad to have me back?" A tanned, but damp, Annette waltzed in.

Carlton and Sheila crushed her with a hug. The last two weeks had been long and arduous and they had missed her company immensely.

It was mid November and Annette was feeling the cold somewhat, having basked in the warmth of the sultry hot sun on her annual break with her husband, but it did not bother her. She had secretly been eager to return to her normal life.

"So how was Lanzarote? You look really well!" Sheila was radiant.

"Great! Apart from the flight going out."

"Here we go!" Carlton was used to her travelling disasters.

"First of all we overslept, but we did manage to catch the flight. When we arrived at the check-in, we were given a note stating that the baggage handlers were on strike at Arrecife and THAT was just the start of it!" She drew in some air. "We got on the plane, but were delayed an hour whilst they fixed the air conditioning. Eventually, we did take off, but almost halfway the pilot announced there was a malfunction — we later found out that it was engine trouble, so we had to turn back and land at Gatwick. The emergency services followed us down the runway. We were stuck on the tarmac for another two hours while the ground crew repaired the engine — it just happened to be the one I was next to. When we finally reached Lanzarote we waited a further hour for our luggage to appear and to top it all off, it was the first day of rain they'd had in six months."

By now, Carlton and Sheila were in stitches. Annette joined in too, but she remembered it was not funny at the time. She had tightly squeezed Julian's hand, until it was white, when they had landed in London and overshot the runway. Annette continued with her holiday highlights. "Things picked up after that, though. The weather was marvellous and the apartment was lovely … By the way, whose is the dummy?"

"What dummy?" Carlton knuckled down to the prep.

"The mannequin at the end of the drive with the staring blue eyes."

"I didn't see a dummy when I arrived this morning. Did you, Sheila?"

"No."

"Go and have a look. It's quite humorous." Annette was grinning.

Carlton returned with a puzzled expression.

"Did you have sun-stroke when you were away? I can't see any dummy."

"Well it was there earlier."

It was almost twelve and a blast of chilly air breezed through the front door.

"Bonjour ladies." Peter was a blonde, amiable man in his mid twenties and was renting the office above the printers. Non-one quite knew what he did, but he popped in for lunch regularly these days.

"Bonjour Pierre." Annette greeted him with a sociable smile. "Comment allez-vous? Tres bien? Oui? Est-ce que je peux prendre votre commande? Salade avec jambon … thon … fromage? Non?"

Peter's face was a complete blank. He held up his hands to surrender, taken aback by the French diarrhoea being hurled at him across the counter. "I haven't the foggiest idea what you're talking about. I only know one word of French." At which point he warily grabbed a pew and picked up the menu.

Annette had ventured on a few short trips to the Continent over the past year. Last May she'd toured the First World War battlefields, around the Ypres area of Belgium and the Somme region of France. Her husband and herself had taken their mothers. Julian's mum, Maggie, was permanently on crutches. She had undergone a hip op, years ago, which had not worked out according to plan. As luck would have it, Annette's Mum, Joyce, had broken her arm and was rigged out with a conspicuous over-the-shoulder sling. Despite resembling the walking wounded of the First World War themselves, they had still embarked on the journey. With sheer determination and deep delving, Annette had, miraculously, tracked down two of her great-grandfathers' graves, one from each side of her family. She had never been able to put into words the emotional relief and comfort she felt at being the first in 85 years to visit their final resting place. They had bought two simple crosses with poppies attached and written a message before compassionately laying them in the soil as a tribute to their ultimate sacrifice. She had been completely overwhelmed by the silent beauty of the immaculate cemeteries, lovingly tended by the local inhabitants. One of the graves had an inscription 'He gave his life for his friends' which had preyed on her mind ever since. She had been in touch with the War Graves Commission and surfed the Internet to try and learn more about how he had died, but all avenues had been exhausted.

More recently, she had treated her mother to a 'Champagne and Chateau' weekend in the serene, lazy countryside of Burgundy. It was a gift to celebrate her mum's 70th birthday. They had toured the vineyards and tasted the wines, relaxed in the inspirationally renovated mansion, adorned with sparkling crystal chandeliers, each enjoying the other's company, but they almost had not made it — the Channel Tunnel had been abruptly closed when salt water had flooded the electrical system.

One of Annette's favourite tours had been to Monet's Water Garden in the charming village of Giverny. She had absorbed the romantic splendour of the flower-filled gardens, ambled along the lavender-lined pathways and savoured the moods and colours of the lily pond in the magical light of the warm, soothing sun. She had also been captivated by the breathtaking canvasses decorating the walls inside the ivy-covered house. A single yellow rose was growing on a trellis beneath Monet's bedroom and she was told that its fragrance would greet him each morning as he surveyed the light. The only regret had been the hotel. It had been absolutely dreadful, but they had not allowed it to tarnish the tour. There was no bar, the room was depressing and one of the waitresses was extremely bolshie. Annette was convinced she only had three words in her tedious repertoire —

"Sorry, not posseebul."

"Can we have more milk, please?"

"Sorry, not posseebul."

"Can we have mayonnaise?"

"Sorry, not posseebul."

When the cantankerous waitress advised them it was "not posseebul" to have dinner on the patio, Annette had snatched up their cutlery, condiments and cloth and set themselves up on a table outside. She would not dream of treating her customers like that.

It was on these trips that she had practised her school French and was eager to brush up whenever the occasion arose, but she had mistakenly believed that Peter could *parlez*. Somewhat disappointed, she obtained his order for quiche in English and laid his table in readiness.

Carlton was smothering his face in his hands. It was Annette's Welsh accent, despite her French name, which constantly creased him up, whenever she indulged in a bilingual *téte-â-téte*. He prepared the quiche and yakked about shares to a ravenous Peter who was ladling French dressing all over his salad. He had returned to his chopping board and was finishing an order when he heard her cheery voice, "*Au revoir, Monsieur*", as Peter retreated back to his office, but he suppressed his amusement whilst he delivered the sandwiches to Table Five.

It was progressively getting busier and busier. Both Annette and Sheila were manically gathering in the orders.

"Two spicy parsnip snoup, please, Carlton." She always had difficulty pronouncing that one and doubled over every time.

When the soup was hot, she cautiously carried it to Table One and kept a close eye on the lady and her husband. She could not believe it when the finely dressed gent, boldly, cupped his bowl in both hands and slurped his soup, licking his lips after every mouthful. She sidled up to a diligent Sheila and helped wrap some knives.

"Any gossip whilst I've been away?"

"Not really. It's been busy in here, but quiet without you." Sheila was so pleased to have her friend by her side again. "Tony and Della have moved out of the main house and into the bungalow. They've swapped with John and Sarah."

That had been on the cards for a while, before Annette had gone away. Tony and Della Brookshaw were handing over the Leisure Park to their son and his wife. She listened to how they had been scurrying, daily, in full view of the coffee shop's kitchen window, lugging boxes and hauling suitcases.

A brief lull cropped up at last.

"I just need to nip to the loo. I won't be long." Annette removed her apron and hurried to the outdoor toilets — the coffee shop was too small to have one of its own. She waved to John and Jenny in 'Applique', the haberdashery and, approaching the ladies, could distinguish an outline through the frosted glass. There would be someone queuing before her, probably one of the craft shop holders. She peeked around the thick, heavy door and there it was — the missing dummy — drying its hands on a paper towel. She hastily 'powdered her nose' and ran back to the kitchen.

"Sheila!"

"Yes?"

"Go to the toilet now!"

"But I don't need to ... I'm doing desserts at the moment."

"Yes you do! Leave them, I'll finish them off."

Sheila gave in and returned in minutes.

"Well? Did you see it?" Annette was flummoxed. A confused looking Sheila snapped back. "See what?"

"The dummy!"

"Oh Annette! You're not still going on about that!"

Annette wiped her brow, perhaps she did have sunstroke, after all.

The coffee shop was chocker by one, but everything was, more or less, under control.

"Has anyone seen my spare chef's overall?" Carlton had spattered himself with curry.

"Have you checked the toilets? The dummy may have stolen it to cover her bits." Sheila mocked loud enough for Annette to hear.

"Tres bonne, Sheila." Annette was a sport.

"Don't you dare go off on that French lark again." Carlton put his foot down for once. Sheila glanced through the window. Someone had caught her eye. She watched Tony Brookshaw, suspiciously, planting a large stuffed seagull on the bonnet of Ricardo Whitley's Porsche. "What's he doing?"

The other two scrambled and perched their chins on Sheila's shoulders as Tony was cagily sneaking away. He only just made it before Ricardo, the owner of the hairdressing salon, appeared at the back, tossing his buttock length locks with his fingers. His dark, dazzling eyes searched the vicinity, but all he discovered was three beaming faces in the coffee shop window.

"Have you done that?" Ricardo gesticulated. Three pairs of eyes shook a prominent 'No'. Ricardo removed a cigarette from his packet and rammed it in the seagull's beak, his body was juddering, restraining his laughter.

Lunches almost done and dusted, Annette escaped to the store room to replenish their stock in the shop. As she opened the lid on the largest freezer, a hand flew up, clouting her sharply across the face. Out of control, she careered into the kitchen.

"C ... Carlton ... Carlton!"

"What is it?"

"There's ... a ... body in the freezer!"

He slammed down the tea towel. "Not again! ... Do you want to lie down?"

"No! Just go and look!"

"Well, if it makes you any happier, I'll put my Inspector Clouseau hat on ..." He trudged into the yard, muttering.

"If you come back and say — 'there is no body', I'll scream." Her rantings followed him.

Carlton was back in the blink of an eye.

"Annette. ...there is no body in the freezer."

"Aaargh!"

"But ... there is a dummy!"

Annette fell silent. She was going to be vindicated after all.

"Who's put that in there?" She adored practical jokes.

Carlton paused. "I think I may have a good idea."

"Who?" Sheila was helpless.

"Possibly our phantom seagull depositor."

Tony was heaving yet another antique suitcase up the gravelled path to his new front door. The attic was almost empty now. He had forgotten about most of the junk which he had collected over the years. Thankfully, there were only a few more boxes to fetch, but he'd been pleased with the pranks that he had conjured up. As he rounded the corner to the front of his bungalow, he was shocked at the sight of a police woman ringing his bell. His heart began to beat, faster and faster, and he slung the suitcase into the bushes, shouting as he advanced on the slim, shapely constable.

"Is anything wrong, officer?"

She stood motionless. He gently touched her shoulder. There was still no movement. He peeked at her face. A wry smile, slowly but surely, began to grow on his genial face. He recognised those staring blue eyes in an instant and only one word flashed into his mind.

"*Touchè.*"

Winter

Mince Pie in the Sky

"Mum! Auntie Netty's here!"

"Don't go running off now, Ben. We don't want any accidents."

Sandra breathed a sigh of relief at the sight of her elder sister striding down the drive, long auburn hair bouncing around her shoulders.

"Morning, Sis." Annette appeared as bubbly as ever, probably blissfully unaware of the mayhem which was undoubtedly to follow, entertaining her three and a half year old nephew. She had not been able to have children and was a novice at child minding, but despite this she loved her niece and nephew as much as she would have adored her own, if fate had been kinder.

It was only a few weeks since the sisters, who had been close since childhood, had lost their father and Annette felt that Sandra needed some time to herself, without having to put on a brave face for the children. So, last Saturday, she'd offered to look after Ben on her day off from the coffee shop, and suggested her sister go and do her last minute Christmas shopping. The in-laws were over the moon to be entrusted with Sandra's other little cherub, 18-month old Devon, for the day.

"Come on then, Ben. Get your coat, it's starting to snow, and you can have a ride in Uncle Julian's posh new car." She winked at Sandra, hugging her affectionately before taking Ben's tiny hand in her own and leading him to her husband's new blue Ford Focus.

"Wave to Mummy!"

Steering her way cautiously down the country lanes, the wipers gently brushed the feathery snow flakes floating on the windscreen. Annette chatted to her VIP — Very Important Passenger.

"Would you like to help me make some mince pies, Ben?"

"Can I take some home for Daddy?"

"Of course you can, and you can tell him you made them all yourself, can't you?"

The little boy grinned, his blue eyes twinkling with growing excitement. Steadily, Annette manoeuvred into her driveway and smiled comfortingly at her sister's little angel, helping him out of his seat belt. He clambered up the mountainous step into the house and galloped to stroke Candy, Auntie Netty's cute tortoiseshell cat.

"Can I give Candy some biscuits please, Netty?" He quite often dropped the 'Auntie' when he was hyper, but he was always polite.

"You can give her a few, but we'll give her a treat when we have lunch. Is that O.K.?"

"Yes." He shouted, running to the cat food cupboard.

She handed him the biscuits and watched him trying to coax her cat into chewing, but Candy was having none of it and turned up her nose, only sniffing the chicken flavoured offerings.

"She's not long had her breakfast, Ben. I don't think she's hungry at the moment. Come on let's put the oven on and start these mince pies."

Ben raced back into the kitchen and helped her to commandeer all the necessary ingredients and baking equipment required for his assignment. Little did his auntie know the utter chaos which was to ensue. First the flour was scattered in every corner you could imagine. It seemed as if the roof had caved in and there were fewer snowflakes outside than in. Water was splattered unceremoniously down most of the pine units and, when the dough was eventually kneaded, there were more bits of pastry plastered to Ben's torso, face and hands than on the pastry board and rolling pin.

Annette was just about to start tearing her hair out when the phone rang.

"How's it going?" Julian's voice chuckled down the line.

"Fine." There was no way she was going to describe the topsy-turvy scene to her husband.

"Can I speak to Uncle Julian?" Ben was pestering and would not give up until he had said his piece to his uncle.

"Ben wants to say hello." She placed the receiver into his pastry encrusted fingers.

"Hello, Ben. Are you looking after Auntie Netty?"

"Yes."

"What have you been doing?"

"Making pastry. Look! I'm all mucky!"

"Yes, I can see that." Uncle Julian lied and was desperately suppressing his laughter.

"Do you know Auntie Netty's been using your car?" Ben was bursting to tell.

"Has she? Thank you for letting me know."

"Say goodbye now, Ben. Uncle Julian has to get back to work." Annette had caught a whiff of burning in the kitchen.

"Bye." Ben was content for the time being.

Regaining the messy receiver, she could hear her husband in stitches.

"I've got … my own … personal spy." He spluttered in between the uncontrollable fits.

"Mm … Can't get away with anything, can I? Good job I didn't invite the window cleaner in!" Somewhat amused he asked,

"Can you pick me up about six, sweetheart? I trust you can survive till then?"

"We'll see. Anyway, must go, the first batch of mince pies are burning. I'll come for you at six then."

She returned to discover Ben cutting out stars with a toy pastry cutter she had purchased in the local supermarket recently.

"Netty?"

"Yes?"

"Mum said Grandad's gone to heaven and he's a star in the sky."

She felt her face flush, she was not sure how Sandra had explained her father's death and Ben was so young, too small to understand. She remembered the numerous occasions when her sister had dropped herself and her mother at the hospital and Ben always thought they were going to take Grandad home to Anglesey, worrying his little head about where he was going to sit as the car was full.

"He's such a thoughtful little boy for three", she contemplated, but she was not sure how her nephew's mind was working and what was coming next.

"That's right, Ben."

"Is heaven further than Anglesey?" he asked, inquisitively.

Obviously, her sister's explanation had not hit home. She could feel a lump in her throat as big as the mound of pastry that was stuck solid in the mixing bowl. Her eyes filled, but she had to be strong and put on the same brave face as her sister must have done when informing Ben that Grandad had died. She lifted him on her knee, sticky fingers clinging to her jumper, but it did not matter. She recollected those loving compassionate words of her father years ago when her own grandad had passed away.

"Heaven is further than Anglesey, my darling. It's a place high up in the sky, further than anywhere you've ever been. You can only see Grandad at night when all the stars are out. He's watching over us, making sure we're all right and as long as we think about him his star will burn brightly, forever shining until we see him again a long, long time from now."

Ben's floury face looked miserable. She tilted his chin upwards.

"Grandad wouldn't want us to be sad. He'd want us to be happy and the happier we are the more his star will shine. So let's finish the rest of these mince pies and get them in the oven."

She quickly wiped the rogue tear from her cheek and gave Ben a teaspoon to spread the mincemeat on his holly and Christmas trees or fling it around the kitchen walls, whatever he decided.

It was around five o'clock when an exhausted Annette delivered a tired, but clean Ben, swinging a carrier bag heaving with various shaped mince pies, back at her sister's.

"Look Mummy! I've made mince pies."

"Have you?" Sandra closed the door sharply, blocking the cold air from the cosy warmth of her home.

"You look whacked, Netty, everything gone according to plan."

"We've had a lovely day, haven't we Ben?"

He nodded, unloading his mince pies one by one on the table.

"This one's for you Mummy, this one's for Daddy, this one's for Devon and this one's for Grandad."

He carefully placed the star shaped mince pie on the end of the line and gently tugged the end of his Mum's skirt.

"Grandad's star will be very very bright tonight Mum … because I'm happy."

Annette turned to her younger sister, her hazel eyes glistening, and they both knew Christmas would be different this year, but Dad would not have wanted them to be sad. His star and treasured memory were better served enjoying the festive season — for him.

The best Christmas present he could ever have was for all his family to be together, happy!

Silver Linings

"Did you get the cling film?" Annette cross-examined Carlton as he shivered through the rear door of the coffee shop, symmetrically balanced by two jam-packed carrier bags.

"Yes, I remembered the cling film?"

"And the sweetcorn?" That was the second item on the list which she had prepared for him yesterday, but he had been blessed with a persistent habit of forgetfulness.

"Yes."

"What about bread rolls … and …?"

Carlton cut her short. "Nag, nag, nag, nag, nag!"

She took no notice and lightened his load, searching for a red pepper in one of the bags.

"Did you buy …?"

"On and on and on!" Carlton interrupted her again, but he knew she would not take it to heart. They had a rapport which was rare between a boss and his staff.

"O.K!" She pretended to be in a strop. "I won't say another word."

Carlton went quiet. He stared at her fake, prim face and couldn't resist. "Did I buy what?"

Annette smiled to herself, chopping the pepper. She could be harmlessly manipulative when she wanted to be. "No, no, doesn't matter."

"I hate it when you do that!"

"Do what?" She knew full well what he meant.

"Never mind … What was I supposed to buy?" Carlton was hooked and wasn't about to let go.

"A Valentine's card for Joanne." She had written it at the top of his list.

The blood drained from Carlton's face. "Er … I didn't forget … I couldn't find one I liked." He was back-tracking fast, but Annette was very aware of the real reason.

"Sheila's in at eleven, isn't she?" Carlton sidled up behind her and peered over her shoulder.

"Yes."

"I may nip out for a while. Can you hold the fort?"

"Of course."

"Thanks Annette. I owe you one."

As Sheila was appearing through the front door, Carlton was disappearing through the back.

"Morning!" Sheila was especially chirpy.

"My word! You're very perky this morning. What's brought this on?"

"I've had a dozen red roses from my darling Phil and he's taking me out for a slap up meal tonight."

"Very nice too. You lucky lady you!" Annette was genuinely thrilled for her.

"What did you get from Julian?"

"Well, he left me a card on my pillow this morning. He usually orders flowers for me, but nothing has arrived yet. You see, we met on Valentine's Day. It's exactly five years today since I went out on the town with my best friend Dawn and we ended up in Scott's Night Club. Julian asked me to dance and it was love at first sight!" She laughed, then continued. "He asked me on a date and treated me to dinner."

"Where's Carlton?" Sheila had just realised he was missing.

"Gone to get a card for Joanne. He forgot, as usual, but he shouldn't be long." Annette carried on chopping, but found herself daydreaming back to the days when she had met her husband. She had had a lodger then and it was a very confused time in her life …

"How was the date last night?" Paul was chewing a piece of lightly buttered toast.

"Great. I had a really good time." Annette was battling with two day's washing up. "We had a drink at Jake's Wine Bar, followed by dinner at that new Spanish restaurant on the main street, El Gomero, I think it's called."

"So what's Julian like?" Paul discarded his empty plate in the soapy water, soaking his trousers in the process.

"He's nice, I like him … easy to talk to and has a sense of humour. We seemed to hit it off and I felt quite relaxed with him." She had no wish to elaborate any further and was not looking for a new relationship. She only wanted to go out, have a good time and a bit of fun. She had fallen in love once and had no intention of being hurt by a man again.

The door bell interrupted their conversation and Annette dried her hands, hurrying to the front door. A massive bouquet of flowers was thrust into her arms by the young boy shuffling on the step.

"Delivery for Annette Francis. Is it your birthday or something lady?"

"N … no." She was stunned. "Th..thank you."

She staggered into the kitchen and all Paul could see was the Garden of Eden on legs. He watched her, bemused, placing them carefully on the table before removing the small white envelope clipped to the cellophane.

"So what does it say?" He was getting impatient.

"Thanks for a wonderful evening. I haven't enjoyed myself so much in a long time. Fancy going to see *Titanic* at the pictures on Friday? Ring you later. Julian."

"My word! You must have made an impression." Paul became suspicious. "Is there anything else you want to tell me?"

"NO!"

He smiled wickedly and she realised he was winding her up.

"You'll need plenty of tissues, you know."

"No I won't. It'll take more than a weepy film to make me cry. I'd be so embarrassed."

She was adamant.

"Right, I'll go and cut your lawns then while you sort out your floribunda."

"Oh, would you? Thanks Paul. You're so good to me."

Annette returned to the sink with her best glass vase and began arranging her flowers. The pale lemon rosette matched the soft cream roses perfectly. She felt tipsy from the fresh aroma, the fragrance of the rust coloured lilies seducing her wistful day dreams. She peered through the kitchen window and watched Paul mowing creative patterns in the garden.

"Is it really almost a year since he'd moved in with her?"

She was working it out. "Yes it must be. Almost twelve months to the day."

They had all been out after work on her best friend Dawn's twenty-eighth birthday. Paul had recently been through a divorce, like herself, and was searching for lodgings.

"I've got a spare room." She had suggested a little warily. They worked well together but sharing a house was a different matter. "We could do a month's trial and see how it goes."

The following weekend Paul was unpacking his belongings when she presented him with a cactus, a gift to make him feel welcome. Naturally, there had been a few teething problems in the early days, sticking to bathroom rotas, using the washing machine, but nothing significant. The worst part had been tolerating the brunt of rumours rife at work, the gossip had spread through all departments like wild fire.

"We're just good friends." They had protested ardently.

"Oh yeah, we've heard that one before ..." eyes insinuating, glances accusing, but they had risen above it and there had been numerous advantages for both of them.

Paul's rent had kept her head above water — she had been struggling with the mortgage since her husband walked out. He was nearer to the office and they saved money sharing lifts, but more than that, they had become close friends, even going 'clubbing' together occasionally on a Saturday night if they were at a loose end. But she had not seen much of him recently. He had met Helen four months ago and she could tell he was smitten. Many a night they had been up till all hours discussing their love lives and confiding their secrets.

The following week dragged for Annette, but Friday surfaced at last. She made Paul drive from work like a madman to give herself enough time to look gorgeous for her date. She tonged her long dark hair meticulously, over and over, and touched up her make-up every two minutes ensuring it was not too much and not too little. "Does this dress look too tight?"

Paul glanced up from the settee.

"You look fine. Stop fussing." He tutted.

She decided to change the subject. She was flapping and needed to calm her nerves.

"Seeing the one and only Helen tonight?"

"No. She's visiting her mother and won't be back until tomorrow."

"So you'll be here when I get back?"

"Yes. Bring Julian in, I need to vet him. Can't have you going out with any Tom, Dick or Harry you know." She thumped him and he winced, clutching his arm, but she knew she had not hurt him, he was teasing her.

Julian was bang on time. She slammed the front door, walked confidently to the car and climbed into the passenger seat smiling. "You look lovely." He complimented her and blushed.

"Thank you. And again, thank you for the beautiful flowers."

She caught a whiff of his aftershave and peeked at him from the corner of her eye.

"Mm … he looks tasty too." She thought.

The film commenced at eight and Julian escorted the woman of his dreams to their pre-booked luxury seats. They had bought wine gums in the foyer. These did not echo around the cinema when you munched them and dignity was amongst the top ten on her list of do's and don'ts when out on a date.

Half way through the picture, her eyes wandered around the auditorium; she had heard sniffling and blubbering, particularly from the five ladies in front, who had all been rummaging in their handbags producing packets of tissues. She felt as if she had a huge lump in her throat, but was determined that she was not going to bawl, it was only a film after all. She sneaked a glimpse at Julian and was astonished to see his green eyes glazed and a solitary teardrop clinging to his bottom eyelashes. She quietly opened her bag, extracted the tissue she had secretly popped in earlier, just in case, and discreetly slipped it into his palm. He lifted his hand and wiped his lids, his lips quivering.

"Are you all right?" Annette enquired, stroking his arm in the car park.

"I should be asking you that. All the people in that cinema were breaking their hearts, except you."

"I don't cry easily since …" She paused, not sure whether to continue.

"Since what?" Julian was intrigued.

"Since my divorce."

She had told him about her ex on their first date, but he had not realised how badly it had affected her. Julian had also been through a broken engagement after a three year relationship. He had been gutted when he found out his fiancé was playing away from home and it had taken time for the wounds to heal.

He chauffeured her home, the perfect gentleman.

"Would you like to come in, my lodger wants to vet you, as he puts it."

"Vet me?"

"It's just a joke, but he would like to meet you."

"O.K. … Vet me?" he muttered under his breath. He had heard about her lodger and at first assumed the same as everyone else but, sensing Annette was genuine, he eventually believed her.

She introduced them and they shook hands. There was football on the telly so they had common ground straight away, discussing their teams and who was going to win the Premiership. She was relegated to brewing the coffee.

"So what do you think of him?" Annette asked after Julian had left. She stared at Paul, waiting for the verdict.

"He's all right, Netty, I approve. He comes across as a decent bloke. I'll let you see him again if you behave yourself."

She laughed, more from relief than from his jesting.

Cruising down the by-pass from work one evening, Paul broached a subject he had been trying to discuss with Annette for days.

"Helen has asked me to move in with her."

She had been expecting this. It was inevitable that one day he would meet the right girl and want to leave. She was inwardly upset, but it was his life and she would never hold him back even though she loved his company. "So when are you leaving?"

"I hope you understand, Netty. We've had a good time together and I'm grateful you helped me when I needed it. I will miss you, loads, but there's nothing stopping us keeping in touch and we'll see each other every day at work. I don't want to leave you in the lurch though. Financially, I mean. I'll give you three months' rent up front to give you time to find someone else."

"Don't be silly. I managed before, I can manage again. I'm happy for you, Paul. Honestly. Good luck to both of you."

"I'll leave next week then."

Next week came all too quickly. Paul came down the stairs, the last box in his arms. As he neared the bottom step she could see his cactus safely lodged with newspaper. This was it then. He hugged her and thanked her for putting up with him for so long and, sadly, she watched him drive away, turning right at the end of the street and out of sight. The house was lonely already, but she fought back those tears clouding his departure, convincing herself there had to be a silver lining. All she needed was a little patience and let each day unfold.

Startled from her deep, thoughtful melancholy, she answered the phone.

"It's Dawn's Mum here. I'm afraid she's been taken back into hospital today. She asked me to let you know."

"Oh no. I'm so sorry to hear that. Is she on the same ward as last time?"

"Yes."

"I'll come and visit her tomorrow afternoon. Thanks for ringing."

Her friend had caught chicken pox nine months ago and it had triggered off a rare rheumatoid arthritis. The attacks disabled her from time to time, so much so that she had to spend a couple of weeks in hospital. Even more downcast, Annette slumped on the couch, head in her hands. The door bell rang, unexpectedly, but she pulled herself together and answered the door. Julian could not stay away from her these days. He sussed something was wrong straight away, her eyes were red and she had obviously been crying, very out of character. She tried to hold back, but overwhelmed she broke down, tears trickling down her disconsolate face.

"What's happened?" Julian was concerned.

She sobbed, gasping for breath and sniffed. "D … Dawn's in hospital, P … Paul's taken his cactus … and … and … Jack died."

He held her tightly in his arms, understanding her completely. Her husband had deserted her for another woman, Paul had left to move in with Helen, her best friend was ill, but he was unsure about Jack. She must think everyone leaves her sooner or later. He took out his handkerchief and lifted her chin towards his face. Gazing into her anxious eyes, he wiped the smudged mascara streaming down her cheeks.

"Look at me, my darling," his voice was calm and soothing.

" Life moves on. It has to. I knew from the second I set eyes on you in the nightclub on Valentine's Day, you were going to be very special to me. You were sitting by the bar with your drink and I was desperate to dance with you. When you said 'Yes' I couldn't believe my luck. You've made me blissfully happy these last weeks. I want you to know that I love you with all my heart and I'll always be there for you."

She was submerged in emotion, but felt safe in his embrace. Deep down she knew she had fallen for him, despite fighting her feelings, but it had all happened so fast. She was afraid to expose her vulnerability, but her heart was telling her they were right for each other. She just needed a little more time before she declared herself.

"Come on, let's have a quiet night in, watch a film and open a bottle of wine." Julian whispered tenderly and they cuddled on the settee for a while until Annette regained her composure.

"There's one thing I don't understand." Julian was puzzled.

"What's that?"

"I know Dawn's not well and Paul's moved in with Helen, but ... who on earth's Jack?"

She smiled sheepishly, knowing full well how foolish she had been, but she answered his question.

"In *Titanic*."

He chuckled, shaking his head. "That must've been preying on your mind for weeks." "Sad isn't it?"

He stroked her shiny hair and kissed her forehead.

"You're priceless you know. Now let's see what's on the box."

He pressed the remote control. The credits were rolling for an old black and white film. KENNETH MORE ... IN ... *A Night to Remember* — the story of the sinking of the *Titanic*.

This time he discreetly slipped his damp handkerchief into her hand. She studied his kind gentle face. "Life moves on." His voice repeated inside her head. Her instincts were cajoling her to commit herself.

"Jules."

"Yes?"

"I love you too."

She had lightly squeezed his hand and all her reservations had melted away as the warmth of his love had sunk in …

Carlton shoved a card under her nose, disrupting her sentimental memories. "Will this do?" He needed a woman's opinion.

She read the verse and gave her approval.

"I've booked a romantic table for two as well."

"Good. Joanne deserves the attention."

It was approaching mid-day and soon their regulars would be trickling in. February was a slow month, but the locals kept their heads well above water. They preferred the peace and quiet of the winter season. Lunches were served with the usual flare and efficiency and as the two effervescent waitresses cleared the tables, an icy gust of wind surged through the front entrance. The poor man delivering the gigantic bouquet struggled to fit through the doorway. Three heads shot up.

"So who's Annette?"

"That's me!" She blushed, attempting to remove them from his soil stained hands and cautiously placing them on their 'chilling out' table. She read the note out loud.

"I love you my little Apple Sunday. Instead of the pictures, I've booked us a restaurant".

"My little Apple Sunday?" Carlton was bent double. Sheila found it quite amusing too, but she was a bit more restrained.

Despite the intense cold of the bright starry evening, the 'Plassey Shippon Restaurant' was packed. Every table was occupied and the romantic ambience filling the air was deeply intoxicating. Adoring couples, sipping glasses of wine, flirted discreetly and the finest champagnes, chilling in sentinel buckets, were being watched over by heart-shaped balloons.

Jeremy, part owner of the restaurant, had guided Phil and Sheila to 'Sox' — each table bore the name of a cow which had lived in that particular stall when the complex was a farm. They had failed to spot Carlton and Joanne seated at 'Daisy' — the cosy table in the corner, feeding each other chocolate terrine around the soothing flame of their candle. They, in turn, were totally oblivious to Julian and Annette who were being escorted to 'Naughty'. Julian scanned the room and noticed Phil on the table next but one. He abandoned his stall, for a brief moment, to shake Phil's hand, then left him and Sheila to enjoy their intimate dinner. He returned Joanne's wave before nodding to Carlton, who was blissfully unaware he had cream on his chin, and hastened back to his alluring 'Apple Sunday'.

As the evening came to a close, the six of them congregated around the bar and Jeremy handed a single red rose to each of the ladies, procuring a kiss in gratitude.

"What a kind man!" Sheila was touched.

"Kind man, indeed!" Carlton smirked. "He only wanted to kiss you all."

"Oh, by the way, Carlton. Did you remember our lottery on your way home?" Annette asked matter-of-factly.

Carlton turned pale and his laughter subsided. The numbers had been drawn two hours ago.

"It's a good job I did then. Isn't it?" She'd reiterated her point yet again, but he would still call her a 'nag' tomorrow. Work would not be the same if he didn't.

Spring

A Lavish Disguise

Annette was busy scrubbing the bird droppings that were stuck solid to the tables outside the coffee shop. It was a pleasantly fresh day, the Easter sunshine was sure to bring masses of holiday makers up to 'The Plassey Leisure Park'.

"Morning Jeremy."

"Morning Annette. I see we're the ones on bird muck patrol again."

Annette liked Jeremy. He was part-owner of the restaurant next door and his sense of humour was accompanied by a 'Sid James' dirty laugh which was very infectious.

She slopped more hot water on a piece of ground-in muck, soaking her apron in the process, and could hear incessant muttering creeping up behind her, getting louder and louder.

"I don't believe it! Some people!"

She wrung out her cloth and lifted her head.

"What's up, Margaret?"

"Someone has stolen the seat from the men's toilet!"

"You're joking! Why would anyone want a used toilet seat?"

"Beats me. But if it's someone's idea of a joke, it's NOT funny."

Margaret had recently won 'Toilet Cleaner of the Year' award and took her duties very seriously. She huffed and puffed towards the caravan site and Annette watched the sprightly, upright figure march into reception.

"Carlton! Sheila!" Annette feigned shock. "There's been a major disaster, I'm afraid. I'm sorry to have to be the one to tell you …"

"What?" Carlton interrupted. He was getting impatient.

"It's especially bad news for you, Carlton. It won't affect me that much, nor Sheila for that matter …"

"Just tell us what's happened!"

"Well … someone … has nicked … the toilet seat from the men's loo."

Carlton and Sheila gasped, but then it clicked what Annette had actually said.

"Margaret's extremely upset" Annette continued between the giggles. "I don't suppose you had anything to do with it?" She stared directly at Carlton, but he held up his hands and took a step back.

"Not guilty."

There was a faint rap on the back door, saving him from further interrogation.

"Jeremy! Missing me already, honey bun?" — Annette wanted to hear that laugh again and she was fond of making him blush.

"I've brought your tickets for the Sixties night tomorrow. There's six here. You're all still coming, aren't you?"

"Yes, we'll be there." Carlton nodded. "Joanne's still working on her outfit, but I'm coming as Elvis, so I won't need to dye my hair."

"Who are you and Phil coming as, Sheila?" Jeremy was curious.

"Sonny and Cher."

"And what about you and Julian, Annette? I can't wait to hear this!"

"John Lennon and Yoko Ono."

"But, but, Julian's got no hair!" Sheila's false look of astonishment was well-timed. The peaceful surroundings were unceremoniously disrupted and their jaws ached from the infection that spread with Jeremy's unmistakeable laugh.

"Have you heard about the missing toilet seat?" Sheila wondered if he could shed any light.

"Yes. Can't imagine who'd want to do such a terrible thing." At which point he made his excuses and returned next door.

Annette switched on the CD system and selected 'play' for the same old disc. Carlton unlocked the front door and it was not long before the customers were pouring in. Yet again, their quaint, little coffee shop was bursting at the seams, but they were quick and nimble on their feet, efficiently serving their hungry patrons. Amidst the short lulls, which rarely presented themselves, Annette and Sheila stacked the baskets ready for the dishwasher, chattering and gossiping, but they never let it interfere with their work.

"Kids O.K., Sheila?"

"Fine. It's Harry's birthday next week and he wants *Play Station 2*. The problem's finding the time to go and get one."

"I know. I went to my niece's fifth birthday last Sunday. There were seventeen kids running around, fourteen boys and three girls, but the magician was excellent. He even had me spellbound."

A woman stormed up to the counter and slammed her fist down, hard, making them jump.

"Everything all right for you?" Sheila regained control of herself.

"The last thing I need when I'm eating my lunch is to listen to you two prattling on about your kids." She threw a fiery glance at each of them. "I've never had children and I never intend to."

"I'm very sorry." Annette apologised. "We didn't mean to upset you."

The woman stomped to the door leaving them reeling, unsure as to what had caused such an outburst.

"It's not worth worrying about." Carlton made an attempt to restore their spirits. "There's always one. You must've hit a nerve or something."

Annette and Sheila soon bounced back and, as bubbly as ever, ensured the well-being of their clientele.

Early afternoon was fast approaching, business was booming and orders were pouring in thick and fast. In fact, everything was going far too well. Lulled into a false sense of security, they were caught unexpectedly when the second calamity pounced.

"Carlton, it's gone very quiet in here." Annette couldn't understand what was missing.

"I've got no cooker, no microwaves. In fact, I've got no power at all. Must've blown a fuse." He, frantically, wrenched plugs out of sockets and switched them around, but nothing. Sheila looked worried. A vein in his neck was beginning to swell and she could see it pulsating.

"What on earth am I going to do? I've still got meals to get out."

As if the situation wasn't dire enough, the burglar alarm leapt into action, blasting out a few thousand decibels, deafening everyone within a thirty-metre radius. The customers were on the edge of their seats, covering their ears, their eyes staring, undecided whether to bolt for the exit or keep calm and stay put.

"Don't panic!" Carlton, hopping mad, yelled at the top of his voice, competing against the high-pitched shrill. At the same time, he was performing his own unique version of a country hoedown, stepping into the middle and back again.

"Don't panic!" He was screaming even louder, but Annette and Sheila ignored his crazed frenzy and carried on coolly as best they could. He stabbed at the buttons on the alarm, but it refused to submit, blaring on and on and on. By now matters were becoming progressively worse. Every car alarm in the car park was being triggered. One by one, like a rippling effect, horns were tooting and people were appearing from all over the place. There were women in curlers tearing out of the hairdressers and ladies in bridal gowns inelegantly sprinting from 'Weddings 'R' Us', hunched up skirts in their arms. All had one goal, to silence their part of the atrocious din.

"I CAN'T REMEMBER THE CODE!" Carlton, at this point, was on the verge of ripping the alarm clean off the wall and the vein in his neck was close to erupting.

"Does anyone else know the number?" Sheila mouthed at him.

He paused for a moment. "MY MUM!" But then he remembered she was in Spain. He snatched his mobile off the fridge and darted out the back. Annette could see him bawling down the phone and recognised one word "LISTEN!" before he held it high into the air so his mum, Irene, could hear the racket for herself. He raced back into the kitchen and flew at the buttons once again.

The subsequent hush was heartily applauded and a crimson faced Carlton executed an elaborate bow. Now he only had to fix the power. He rummaged in the 'bits box' and pulled out a fuse.

Sheila, meanwhile, was doing a good job perking up the diners.

"Not keen on the new CD, are you? Head banging's not my scene!"

"Can I order now?" The second misery of the day was on table three.

Finally, the last customer paid his dues and Carlton locked the door behind him. He slumped on their usual table and Sheila poured three strong coffees. It was their way of unwinding after a long, hectic day.

"My ears are still ringing." Annette took a sip. "I hope tomorrow's easier." She was pooped, but she still had to go home and sort out a Yoko Ono outfit for the Sixties do the following night.

Easter Saturday, and it was bright and sunny for the second day in a row. A cheerful Annette bumped into the cleaner outside the ice-cream parlour.

"Morning, Margaret. Has the gent's seat turned up yet?"

"No, it hasn't! But don't you worry, I'll get to the bottom of it, if it's the last thing I do."

She strode in the direction of the lavatory, bucket and mop swinging erratically. Itching to get into work to up-date her companions, Annette hurried into the shop, amused.

"What's tickled you?" Carlton was hacking a cabbage for coleslaw and Sheila was peeling the carrots.

"I've just seen Margaret and she's determined to get to the *bottom* of the missing toilet seat."

Their hysterics were cut short by a big, white van reversing into the rear yard.

Sheila peered through the window. "Milko's here."

"Hi, Alan." She unlatched the door. "How are you today?"

An invisible peg was pinching his nose. "Gotta cold."

"Keep your distance then, I don't want it." She was full of sympathy.

Carlton extracted some money from the till. "We need three large milk, one cream and a dozen eggs, please." Milko scribbled on his pad, wiped his nose and sniffled to his van. He left the items on the step and mumbled, "See you," before heading next door.

Annette, having popped the milk in the fridge, straightened up to serve the customers shuffling at the counter.

"Gut morning." The leader grinned, displaying a row of yellow buck-teeth.

She knew they were German. She'd learnt languages at school.

"How can I help you?"

"Ve vant ze Velsh cream tea. Ja?"

"Ja." She kept a straight face despite spotting Carlton from the corner of her eye leaning over the sink, shaking.

"Where would you like to sit?"

"Ve vill zit in ze garden. Ja?"

"Ja." She smiled sweetly. "I'll bring it out for you."

"Danke."

She bided her time until the Germans had disappeared, picked up a tea towel and slapped Carlton several times.

"I'm so sorry, Annette, I couldn't help myself … It was your wonderful German accent that finished me off … but a word of advice. When you take out their 'Velsh cream tea' — DON'T MENTION THE WAR."

With a pot of tea for six, homemade scones, jam and freshly whipped cream, Annette and Sheila carted the trays into the garden, despite it being a little early in the day for afternoon tea. One of the foreigners slipped out a cam-corder and aimed it directly at them. Annette whispered, "Und zese are ze little Velsh vaitresses vit ze Velsh cream tea." She continued her commentary through clenched teeth. "Ja, Sheila?"

"I'd pray they can't lip read if I were you. Remember they'll be playing back the video when they go home."

"Is there anything else you'd like?" Annette enquired placing the last cup and saucer on the table.

"Nein, danke. Zis is gut. Ja?" He gestured at the faraway hills, the landscape was absolutely breathtaking on clear days and the blossoming scenery was a sight to behold.

"Ja, wunderbar." She resisted the urge to click her heels and followed Sheila with the empty tray.

Carlton was leaning against the dessert cabinet as she returned through the kitchen door. He was grinning from ear to ear, shaking his head. Annette never ceased to amaze him.

"Are they happy out there?"

"Ja wöhl, mein herr!" Annette rolled her eyes and followed through with the empty tray to clear table one.

Another tiring day sailed by swiftly, but they skipped their normal routine, rushing home to get ready for the dance.

The restaurant was buzzing when John Lennon and Yoko Ono, Sonny and Cher and Elvis, with Dusty Springfield on his arm, namely Joanne, strolled in. Dusty was precariously balancing an enormous beehive on her head and had glued spidery false lashes to her lids. Jim Reeves, alias Jeremy, surged forward to greet them and escorted them to their favourite table —'Naughty' — the name of the cow which had inhabited that stall in the days when the restaurant was a cattle shed.

"We've got some special entertainment for you later," Jeremy was excited and paused to draw breath, "and I've hired professional rock 'n' roll dancers. They should be arriving any minute. Can I get you any drinks?"

Phil ordered a round of Cherry Bs and lagers, drinks from the swinging Sixties, but much to his disappointment, they cost present-day prices.

Joanne was tapping her feet and strumming her fingers to *Living Doll*. "Sheila? I mean, Cher?"

"Mm?"

"Your mum and dad babysitting for Harry and Amy?"

"Yes. I left Amy planning Harry's birthday. She absolutely loves arranging parties, you know. She's colouring in a banner she's made to hang on his bed." Sheila was so proud of her kids.

"Bless her."

Their conversation was put on hold as the hired dancers took centre stage. The music was lively and thunderous and everyone clapped, enjoying the up-beat performance.

Carlton, relaxed for a change, was about to swallow his first gulp of beer when, out of the blue, a female rock 'n' roller with exuberant red lipstick, seized hold of his hand. She dragged a reluctant Elvis on the floor. She pushed him backwards then pulled him forwards, twirling and spinning. Suddenly, her petticoats surrounded his waist, but his lightening reactions caught her expertly under the arms, before she lunged her legs backwards and sprang back on the floor, feet perfectly together.

"Now swing me around your shoulders!" She shouted breathlessly above the vigorous beat.

"What?" The look of horror on his face was apparent, but in the nick of time, Joanne astutely slalomed a course, dodging in and out of the dancers, and nuzzled between them. The female, hands on hips, raised an eyebrow, but seemingly unbothered, sloped off on the prowl for another victim. "Thank you so much, sweetheart." He wheezed at Joanne.

"You looked like you needed some help." She noticed he had lost one of his sideburns, but opted not to let on. It wasn't often she could get one up on him.

Everyone took their seats for the highlight of the evening. Frank Sinatra, better known as Gavin — the head chef, strutted up the stage steps to make the introductions.

"Tonight, ladies and gentlemen, we have a very special treat in store for you. Allow me to present our very own skiffle band. We have Jim Reeves on the washing board," that was Jeremy, of course, "Clarke Gable playing the banjo with his lovely wife, Doris Day on the spoons," otherwise known as Neil and Beverly — Jeremy's business partners, "and the fabulous Marilyn Monroe live on the tambourine." Vicky, the restaurant manager, was dolled up to the nines and a blast of cold air wafted up her dress. "Ladies and gentlemen, I give you — 'The Lucky Jim Band'."

Wolf whistles and cheers welcomed them as they tuned up quickly and launched into a superb rendition of *My Old Man's A Dustman*.

Carlton was definitely getting in the mood, stamping his feet and thumping the table. He studied the horseshoe shaped sign suspended above the stage, the band's name painted in black letters. He stared at it, his mind ticking over.

"Anything wrong?" Annette nudged him in the ribs.

"That sign up there." He pointed.

"Yeah? What about it?"

"It's vaguely familiar. Can't help thinking I've seen it somewhere before."

Annette took another glimpse. "Can't say I've seen it anywhere, but it reminds me of ... "

They swung to face each other and in synchronized harmony, exclaimed.

"A TOILET SEAT!"

"Good job Margaret's not here." Annette's slanted eyes explored the room just to make sure, not that she'd recognise the cleaner amongst all the celebrities, but she found herself searching for a Hilda Ogden look-alike.

The next day, a thick-headed Annette could hear someone calling her across the yard as she headed for the rear of the coffee shop .

"Yoo, hoo! Annette! Annette!"

She laboured to manoeuvre her sluggish head. Margaret was waving, dashing towards her.

"You'll never guess what's re-appeared?"

Annette was not in the mood for games.

"What's that?"

"The men's' toilet seat … I went in there to clean this morning and there it was, just sitting there as if nothing had happened."

Annette managed a feeble smile, but her mind was preoccupied, speculating on how long it had taken Jim Reeves to clean off 'The Lucky Jim Band'. No wonder he had been on bird muck duty so often, lately. He had been getting in plenty of practise.

Operation Dessert Fox

D Day. 6th June. Carlton's birthday:

19.55 hours:
"SURPRISE!"

Carlton ricocheted off the restaurant door and was dazed by the troops assembled in reception. He had sensed that something was up all day, but could not quite put his finger on it.

10.12 hours: Earlier that day.

Annette nipped into the doughcraft shop, to requisition a card for Carlton. She had bought his present weeks ago, but it was not until she was wrapping it the previous evening that she remembered she needed a card. She found Martin in attendance, his wife Jackie was away at a craft fair. They were both used to her dashing in, last minute, begging them to rescue her from forgetful embarrassment, but it was the only thing she was a little lax on. He helped her to choose an appropriate design, a chef made of dough with a wicked grin on its face. He inscribed a message, placed the card in a bag and she hurtled through the door to open up the coffee shop.

10.30 hours:

Carlton's two loyal lieutenants were, staunchly, washing and preparing the salads in readiness for the bombardment at lunchtime. He meandered through the rear door and graced them with his presence on his special day, clasping a bundle of envelopes addressed to Mr C. Fox. They were obviously cards he had been handed making his way into work.

Annette and Sheila pecked him on the cheek, wished him a "Happy birthday" and off-loaded their presents. He unwrapped Sheila's first, scrunched the paper and tossed it into the bin. It was a metal maze type game. The trick was to manoeuvre the coffee pot through the correct channels to the centre and fill the static china cup and saucer without spillage. He thought it was cool.

He was a little more cautious opening Annette's having had the pleasure of her gifts in the past. They had this ritual of buying each other the tackiest present they could root out on their holidays. She had come back from Amsterdam with a silver coloured lighter. The woman's boobs glowed and flashed every time he lit a ciggy. He had returned the favour with an African leopard skin thong from the deserts of Tunisia, no mean achievement.

He discarded the holographic paper and was not disappointed. She had bought him a key ring with a rubber nose attached. He squeezed it, apprehensively, and green plastic goo dribbled out. They roared as he checked out the second part of his gift, an antique book detailing the history of the R.M.S. *Mauretania*. He was over the moon. Carlton had transformed his dining room at home into a sort of shrine to the great ship. He had managed to lay his hands on an original pair of swing doors via the internet. The *Mauretania* had been scrapped in 1935 and all the fixtures and fittings had been auctioned off at Southampton Docks, a sad end to a brave ship which had transported troops during the Gallipoli campaign of 1915. The doors were now adorning the entrance of his own cosy eating room. He had hammered up shelves creating the atmosphere of a ship's library and spent numerous Sundays, up at the crack of dawn, scouring car boot sales for old archetypal books in pristine condition.

Annette and Sheila received a big bear hug and, still chuckling over the key ring, plodded on with the food.

Carlton answered the phone.

"Stables Coffee Shop … Hi, Jimmy … Thanks … O.K. up to now …Hang on, I'll just ask Annette." He placed his hand over the receiver. "Annette?"

"Yes, birthday boy?"

"D'you think you could manage without me on Saturday? Jimmy T's on, he wants to take me to the game, my birthday treat."

"Yes. No probs."

"That's fine, Jimmy. I'll see you at two then."

Carlton was an avid football fan. Most people supported Man United, Everton or Leeds, but not Carlton. Oh no. His team was Chester City F.C. There were so few spectators at their matches Carlton was worried that, one day, he would be on *A Question of Sport*. He had nightmares about the ball being kicked wildly into the crowd, consisting of only himself and Jimmy, and he would have to toss it back on the pitch, making a complete and utter hash of it. He dreaded ending up on the 'What happened next?' round.

To be fair to him, though, he never wavered in his commitment and seized every opportunity to go to their games. He was used to the leg pulling and, lately, his club were playing brilliantly. He would have the last word when his team gained promotion at the end of the season.

10.55 hours:

Carlton had hacked the cheese into chunks and was reaching for the shredder. The plug became caught between the microwaves and the hard plastic bowl crashed to the floor. They all heard the crack as the handle split.

"Blast!" He was cross. They needed the cheese grated ready for lunch. The only solution was the superglue. He raided the 'bits box', detected the tube and stuck the handle back to the bowl. He was so proud of himself until, he suddenly realised, he had also bonded his index and middle fingers together.

"Annette?"

"Yes?"

"Um … Um."

"Come on. Spit it out."

He displayed his two fingers, fused solid.

"Is that a new version of a rude gesture or something?" She was unsure what he was doing.

He bit his lip. "They're superglued."

At that precise moment, Sheila was dispatching more dishes for washing and glanced at Annette who was also biting her lip, but not for the same reason as Carlton. She was dieing to laugh, but then began to digest how disastrous the situation could become. He could not go to the hospital. If he was 'stuck' there for hours, he would miss his party. But, on the other hand, he couldn't turn up at the restaurant next door with two fingers firmly glued together.

Sheila organised a bowl of hot water with washing up liquid and made him soak them for almost five minutes. He removed his wrinkled fingers and strained to part them, but the opposite was happening. They were getting tighter and tighter. Annette and Sheila watched the panic unravelling on his face and when he could not stand it any more — "There's only one thing for it." He removed the razor blade from the coffee bag cutter and proceeded to prise his fingers apart.

Annette and Sheila grimaced and cringed. His Mum, Irene, would have their guts for garters if he arrived at the party with no fingers at all. The relief on his face confirmed his success and his waitresses sighed, relieved for a different reason. He spent the rest of the day picking at the bits until his fingers were completely clear.

"That was a close call." Sheila murmured to Annette.

"You can say that again."

13.05 hours:

"Salut, Pierre." Annette liked to joke with Peter since the day she'd spurted her French at him.

"Mange Tout, Annette." He ribbed.

She waited for his order, the amusement illuminated in her eyes.

"I'll have curry today, please, and a glass of water."

"Certainly. Thank you." She lowered her voice. "Are you still going to the party tonight?"

"Yes. Should be a laugh. I can't wait to see his face."

She dispatched the order to Carlton.

"What were you two whispering about?" He extracted the rice from the freezer. She had to think quickly. "You!"

"Very funny!"

By telling him the truth, she had avoided his probing and rushed to clear Table Two.

13.25 hours:

Three breaths of fresh air wafted through the door. Annette's favourite ladies 'The Jolly Girls' met every Thursday for lunch. They had a soft spot for Table One and could have a laugh and a natter with the waitresses. Lunch in the coffee shop was always enjoyable. It was the one thing they looked forward to every week. Annette had estimated they were all in their thirties, one she knew was a farmer's wife and the other two were, so called, ladies of leisure, but taking care of husbands can be a full time job.

"Hi! How are you all today?"

"Fine, thank you, Annette."

"Coffee while you're deciding?" She was fully conversant with their eating habits.

"Yes please."

"With the usual dash of arsenic?"

The 'Jollies' cracked up. Annette was skilful at weighing up the customers that she could tease and tantalise and those that she could not. The homely atmosphere was ablaze with hysterics and as soon as they discovered it was Carlton's birthday, the incessant jokes about age cascaded.

14.38 hours:

'The Jolly Girls' settled their bill, their jaws aching from laughing rather than eating, and left their usual generosity in the tips tray.

"See you next week, ladies." Sheila politely showed them the door.

16.40 hours:

Annette was preparing to mop her floor as soon as they closed.

"So, what are you up to tonight, Carlton?" Sheila was curious to know what yarn he'd been spun.

"Joanne's taking me next door for a quiet, intimate dinner."

"Very nice." She smirked, placing a clean bag in the bin.

17.05 hours:

The door had been locked and three steaming coffees had been placed on Table Five.

"I can't stay long. I'm babysitting for Ben and Devon tonight. My sister has to work."

It was the best excuse Annette could come up with.

"No, nor me." Sheila joined in. "Phil's going out with the lads, leaving me with the kids."

They both wanted to get home quickly to tart themselves up for the party, but did not want Carlton to become suspicious. They drank their coffee, wished Carlton a good time and headed briskly for their cars.

19.32 hours:

Annette, Julian, Sheila and Phil arrived together in a taxi. Crimson suited Annette. Her outfit accentuated her dark eyes and hair, her curls flowing around her shoulders. Sheila's short length, satin blue dress was incredibly eye-catching and she was gorgeous as usual. Their men had made an enormous effort to compress themselves into their James Bond attire. Jeremy's eyes almost popped out of his head. He was not used to seeing chic, stylish waitresses from next door. He normally encountered them in white, unflattering shapeless blouses partly concealed with green check aprons. The foursome had a shock too, Jeremy looked ravishing kitted out in a black dinner jacket and perfectly knotted bow tie.

"Evening, hun." Annette could not resist missing an opportunity to make him redden.

19.57 hours:

Carlton was recovering from the bombshell. He was a sitting duck, nowhere to run. Irene and Raymond, his parents, were on the front line. He trundled through the barrage, shaking hands and planting kisses, steadily aiming for the alcohol. His own platoon were propping up the bar.

"What'll you have, Carlton?" Phil was in the middle of reeling an order to Beverly manning the pumps.

"Lager, please."

His battalion of weekend staff rallied to surround him. They had clubbed together to buy him a genuine leather wallet. The one he had was falling apart. Annette would have said 'moth eaten', if she had been around at that point.

"Thanks, girls." He was revelling in the attention.

Samantha and Laura introduced their boyfriends.

"This is 'Big Dave', Carlton." Sam was proud of her date.

Carlton stared at his massive, muscular chest and steadily gazed up. Dave was big all right, built like a Sherman tank, and his hand shake was crushing.

"Wouldn't want to meet him in a dark alley." He mumbled to Joanne, flinching. Laura's other half was the total opposite. Short, slim and a meek personality.

20.30 hours:

Jeremy announced that dinner was served and he escorted the coffee shop staff to 'Naughty'. Carlton, as guest of honour, was seated at the head of the table. Hydrogen filled balloons floated all around him. They had been tied to his chair with rainbow coloured ribbons and birthday confetti had been spirally strewn, reflecting the magnificent arrangement of pure cream freesias and deep golden roses.

The Brookshaws had turned out in force and were seated, adjacent, on 'Sox'. They wielded their glasses and swigged their drinks. "Iechid Da!" was the battle cry toasting Carlton's health.

Ricardo, flamboyantly dressed in a frilly silk shirt, with his lovely wife Claire were on the other side. Peter had joined them. He had been unable to secure a baby sitter, so unfortunately, his wife could not make it.

The restaurant staff proficiently served a fabulous first course of Normandy paté with homemade apple chutney and melba toast. Operation 'Dessert Fox' was in full swing. The room was buzzing with laughter and chit chat and Carlton was accepting beer after beer. The next course, cooked to perfection, consisted of a sumptuous beef Wellington, baby roast potatoes and deliciously crisp, fresh vegetables.

Before dessert, Carlton was called upon to make a speech and begrudgingly rose to his feet.

"All I want to do is thank everyone for coming tonight … hic … and thank you to my mum, dad and Joanne for arranging this surprise … hic …" His eyes were orbiting and his legs were wobbling. He toppled backwards and crash-landed on his chair. Julian and Phil just managed, between them, to prevent his chair tipping over, but he would not have felt the impact anyway.

The chocolate bombe rations were paraded to the tables with Vicky, the restaurant manager, leading the way. Two of the coffee shop's Saturday girls, Sarah and Lucy, were confessed chocoholics and their youthful faces lit up when their plates were set down. They tucked in devotedly and did not surface until the bombe had completely disappeared. Close inspection of their chins and noses revealed that an explosion must have occurred somewhere between the first and last mouthfuls.

22.14 hours:

The coffee cups were being cleared and Jeremy made his second announcement.

"Ladies, Gentlemen and Carlton … If you would all like to return to the bar, we can clear the floor and the dancing can commence."

Scraping chair legs and clip-clopping stilettos spread through the dining area as the guests vacated their stalls. They continued their gossiping, equipped with champagne and filed into the lounge area.

22.20 hours:

Jeremy had become the makeshift D.J. The one he had booked having let him down at the last minute. He was the only option. Neil and Gavin were crucial to the kitchen, Beverly was vital at the bar and Vicky was essential to the clear up.

Stevie Wonder began the proceedings. "Happy birthday to you. Happy birthday to you. Happy birthday …"

Joanne led Carlton to the dance floor. He was, by now, experiencing immense difficulty with his co-ordination and boogied on down like Bambi on an ice rink. So, when he stumbled, in slow motion from the flashing strobes of disco lights, disarming 'Big Dave' of his pint, the room fell silent. Everyone gasped, waiting for the flare-up and possible combat. Carlton was still giggling when Dave lifted him up by his armpits. The fact that there was air between the floor and his feet meant nothing to him at all. He carried him over to the nearest seat and dumped the dead weight down, forcefully.

"There you go, mate. I think you'll be safer sitting there." Dave brushed himself down with a serviette left on one of the tables, and marched to the bar for another bitter. The relief reverberated in every corner and gradually the party animals picked up the pace, grooving and celebrating until the early hours.

To Carlton, it was the 'Longest Day'.

11.40 hours: D Day +1 — 7th June. Carlton's hangover.

A pair of dark glasses on a pale white face stumbled through the back door of the coffee shop. Annette and Sheila had everything under control and offered the sheet a cheery "Good Morning".

"Keep your voices down, if you don't mind!" Carlton felt ill.

He stretched out on the long cushioned seat under the window and removed his sunglasses. His eyes were on stalks, bloodshot and puffy.

"Do you think you'll last the day?" Sheila was mildly sympathetic.

"Don't know."

"Carlton. I'm not sure whether I should make up more salads?" Annette was uncertain whether forty were enough and was hoping for guidance.

"Do what you like!"

Sheila noticed a coach parking up and it appeared to be full. They were not expecting a party, but sometimes they did turn up out of the blue. She nudged Annette, who looked up to the heavens.

"Carlton?" Annette was trying to break the news gently.

"What?"

"SURPRISE! THERE'S A COACH IN!"

Summer

A Wild Country 'T'

"Overslept, have we?" Annette noticed instantly that Carlton was wearing his T shirt inside out. The seams and the label had provided a clue.

"How do you know? I'm not late, am I?"

She glanced at the clock. It was ten precisely.

"No, just a lucky guess, I suppose." Her wind-up of the day had been presented on a plate. She was loading her gun.

"Did you watch Tim Henman last night?" She rapidly changed the subject, distracting his thoughts as to how she'd hit the nail on the head.

It was the middle weekend of Wimbledon fortnight and for once the weather was dry, but there was a down side. The coffee shop was quieter and would be for another week, especially as the Brits were playing well, but they did have three coach parties down in the diary to tide them over, the first of which was booked in at four.

It was humid already and Carlton, unable to cope, moseyed over to the front door, wedging it open with an iron weight to allow some air to flow in. Annette was occupied in the kitchen, skilfully quartering the red skinned tomatoes, whilst Sheila was choosing a well worn CD. *Raindrops keep falling on my Head* was piping through the speakers when Jane, Sheila's sister, appeared at the back. Her head in the clouds, she tripped, head first, and shot over the doorstep, two freshly baked cakes in each hand.

"Wo! Wo!" Carlton managed to save them.

Jane was unbelievably accident prone, so much so, Annette had affectionately dubbed her 'Calamity'. She was, however, the most fabulous cook. Her Victoria sponge was incredibly moist and her melt-in-the-mouth coffee cake was a huge favourite with the customers.

"Phew! That was close!" Carlton, relieved, hurried to the till to settle with Jane before she had any more mishaps. As she was leaving, the cavalry was arriving. Little Jo and Eleri always came to the rescue on their busiest day of the week.

"Hi, girls!" Carlton ushered them in and dispensed two aprons.

Both were very pleasant teenagers studying for their GCSEs. Carlton, Annette and Sheila spoiled them rotten, but they were keen to work and respected their elders. They loved their Saturday job, but Annette often worried about the sharp awakening which awaited them in the big, wide world of employment.

"Your Auntie Gwyn's in, Annette." Little Jo flicked her plaits and a loosely tied bow slipped out.

Ditching the knife, Annette washed her hands and discovered her aunt on table three. "Morning! How are you?"

"Fine, thanks. I'm killing some time before my hair appointment and thought I'd have a coffee while I'm waiting."

Ricardo and Claire rented the premises above and ran a very successful hairdressing salon. Many of their clients nipped into the coffee shop before or after their appointments — particularly the ladies, who never felt intimidated walking in on their own. The proprietor and waitresses were so friendly and affable. In fact, they even looked forward to the entertainment. Anything could happen.

"I've bought a new car." Auntie Gwyn continued.

"What is it?"

"A Vauxhall Vectra. It's a saloon."

"Very nice too."

Carlton delivered the coffee and, as he spun round, Auntie Gwyn detected the label on his shirt prominently displaying 'L'. She was about to enlighten him when Annette grasped her hand.

"Don't say a word." She prevented her aunt from spilling the beans. She was reining him in, bit by bit.

They both snugly laughed and her aunt shook her head. She understood her niece so well. Their private gossip was cut off in its prime as they both weighed up the dodgy butch hombre swaggering up to the counter.

"Well, hello there, Clayton! Long time no see, deary!" His voice was as sweet as the sugar on the tables and was not compatible with his appearance at all.

Carlton, who was currently on his first diet, unfortunately, was caught red-handed. He was clutching a flowery paper handbag which Sheila had given him, containing reams of weight watching info. He shuffled uneasily. He recognised the face, but could not remember the name. "All right? … " It, gradually, dawned on him. "Keeping well?"

"Mm … Not bad, you know. I was in the neighbourhood, lovey, and decided to call for a coffee, black please."

"This is my diet bag." Carlton felt obliged to fill him in.

Eleri sorted the order and Annette breathed in, squeezing passed her into the kitchen. She'd overheard and whispered to Carlton. "Friend of yours? CLAYTON!"

He winced. "Jumping the gun again, Annette! He's just somebody my Mum and Dad met on holiday. I think his name's Lance."

High noon and the punters were coming in droves. Little Jo and Eleri were run ragged by a grandma and daughter with three marauding kids. There was the spilt orange to wipe, the eternal pestering to pander to, as well as mopping the dripping ice-cream. Carlton's deputies concentrated on the garden. Sheila adored the summer as much as Annette, especially on balmy, warm days like today. Yes, it did get unbearably hot in the kitchen, but she was an optimist and thought of the calories she was burning, whipping around the shop and the grounds. The views were astounding, whatever the time of year. The hazy ridged mountains were barely visible and only a lonesome white cloud scarred the sky. Yonder, a hefty bull was sitting near the creek, panting and snorting in the intolerable heat. A crow was perched on the fence post beyond, squawking noisily blemishing the peace. Spurred on by a mob herding in through the front, she dashed inside to handle the onslaught.

Carlton was scribbling an order on five. He could hear something buzzing. It sounded like a wasp, but there was nothing to see. There it was again. Something tickled his neck and slid down his back. He threw down the order pad, tore off his T shirt and stamped on it over and over. When he'd finished his war dance, he picked it up, shook it and the flattened wasp plummeted to the floor.

Annette was startled by the commotion. "Carlton! What's going on?" A bare-backed Carlton was fiddling with his shirt, which was now right side out, but he threaded the sleeves through the neck and slipped it back on, the seams were protruding yet again.

"There was a wasp in my shirt and the darn thing's stung me." He was trying to be brave and exhibit true grit. Table five were gawping with shock, but Annette smoothed it over.

"Have you seen the Chippendales before?"

She scouted around for the insect bite cream and tapped Carlton on the arm. He was hanging up a tea towel, but took the tube and doctored his wound. He scrubbed his hands and carried on with the meals.

"I'm running low on sweetcorn."

"I'll fetch some." Annette was ambushed on her way to the store room.

"I'm organising a barn dance for next month. Interested?" Jeremy was testing the water.

"Yes. Sounds like fun. I'll have a word with Carlton and Sheila."

Late afternoon was upon them and Sheila was industriously dishing out saucers, preparing for the 'Gold Rush of 52' — that is fifty-two pensioners with gold coloured dentures.

"She reminds me of a croupier," Annette nudged Carlton, "dealing a pack of cards.

She'll leave the last saucer for you."

"Why?"

"It's a joker!" She sneaked another glimpse at the label on his top. She'd thought the gag had back fired earlier, when he'd ripped it off turning it right side out.

"The coach is here!" Sheila retreated to the safety of the kitchen with a single left-over saucer. She discarded it with a thud, directly in front of Carlton.

"Told you!" Annette raised an eyebrow. Carlton was confused, he wasn't on her wavelength, but there wasn't time to chew it over, the stampede would be trampling and hustling in seconds.

The raiding party rolled in. They were a tribe from Deganwy, brandishing walking sticks and spitting feathers. They were on the last stage of their mystery tour and had spent much of the day staked out in their seats with the searing sun penetrating the windows.

Annette and Sheila were behind the barricade. They'd been volunteered to control the orders, chucking them back to Carlton and the girls.

"Two teas and two Welsh cakes." The old dear's war paint had started to smudge.

"So, that's two teas and two Welsh cakes." Annette never gambled, repeating the orders to ensure they were right.

"What's that, cariad?"

"I said two teas and two Welsh cakes." She raised her voice slightly.

"You'll have to speak up, I can't hear you."

"TWO TEAS AND TWO WELSH CAKES."

"No. I want two teas and two Welsh cakes."

"TAKE A SEAT AND WE'LL BRING IT FOR YOU."

The next in line were obviously brothers. Both had been scalped and had smoky grey eyes.

"Four coffees, two scones and a caramel shortbread."

Yet again, the order was recapped. A voice floated over the heads at the front.

"I've changed my mind, Bill. I will have a scone."

"OK, Coral … make that three scones, not two, please."

Annette changed the order.

The vacant space was swallowed up by a mean-looking stranger with an axe to grind.

"I've been waiting ages for my coffee and teacake!" Annette checked his claim. It was in Carlton's hands.

"I'm so sorry. Your order is being dealt with now. I'll bring it over in a minute."

Twenty-nine teas and twenty-three coffees later, Annette distributed the bills to each table. The lady who had ordered the Welsh cakes for two was engrossed in a pow wow on Table One. She tugged Annette's apron, seeking attention.

"Can I pay you, please, cariad?"

"Certainly. That'll be £3.40." Annette pointed at the amount on the tab.

"This is Sue. It's her birthday." She placed a caring hand on her friend's arm. "She's a magnificent seventy-one today."

"Happy Birthday! Have you had a good day?" Annette showed an interest and listened to how they had been on the trail since eight that morning on a scorching bus, their lunch was awful and they wished they had eaten here instead. They'd drifted the plains around North Wales, but now they were exhausted and could not wait to get home.

Meanwhile,

"We're desperately short of change, Carlton." Sheila was holding yet another £20 note to pay for a £1 coffee.

"Glyn might have some tenners and fivers to spare. I'll go and see." He sprinted to the caravan site food store. The owner, Glyn, had a knack of accumulating a wad of various notes and was especially good at hoarding £1 coins.

Carlton charged back into the shop with a fistful of change and helped Sheila to quash the uprising.

As soon as the driver had downed his free tea, he rounded them up and moved them on out, marshalling them back to the stifling coach. Annette and Eleri waved them goodbye with no reservations whilst the coach headed west into the sinking sun, a cloud of dry dust billowing behind.

"This place looks like a battlefield." Annette helped Sheila to load the trays and gather the strewn serviettes. She delegated the washing up by passing the buck to Jo and Eleri. Their big chief, Carlton, was left unfettered to wildly continue patting his sting.

Not a moment too soon, the front door was locked and Little Jo and Eleri were thanked with their pay. Sheila poured three glasses of fresh orange juice. It was far too hot for coffee today and, instead of flaking out on their favourite table, they each grabbed a seat in the shaded gazebo.

"Carlton?"

"Yes, Annette."

"There's something I've been meaning to tell you all day." Her finger was on the trigger.

"Oh yes and what's that?"

"Your T-shirt's inside out."

"What!" He tugged the collar and twisted around. "You could've said something earlier. Anyway, there's something I've been meaning to tell you all day."

She peered at him, baffled.

"You've been wearing odd earrings."

She could tell as soon as she touched them they differed.

Carlton had turned the tables adeptly and he wrenched off his shirt, pulling it right side out, before yanking it back over his head.

Sheila fell silent, glaring at her feet. "Anything wrong?" Annette enquired.

"You're never going to believe this … I've only just realised …" She bit her lip. "but my shoes don't match!"

Carlton and Annette inspected her feet. It wasn't blatantly obvious, as both were the same design, but one was definitely black and the other dark navy. The three amigos howled for ages. Carlton was shattered. He picked up his empty glass and neatly placed his chair under the table. "I'll just ring Joanne, before I go home and catch up on the tennis."

Annette and Sheila wearily analysed the imprint of a burly black foot on his back, about a size ten, as he strolled towards the rear of his empire.

Annette finished her drink and collected the laundry. She said her farewells and, biting the bullet, climbed into her steaming hot car. She, automatically, followed the arrows to the exit and selected a CD — *Hits of the 70s*. She braked at the junction, adjoining the main road, and sang along to a group called 'The Sweet'.

"Wigwam bam …"

Evans Above!

"I need a life." Annette, bleary-eyed, dropped in a ruck at Table Five next to Sheila.

"And me," Carlton agreed, "all I do lately is eat, sleep and work."

It was closing time at the coffee shop, August Bank Holiday Monday. All three of them were completely and thoroughly whacked having worked eight straight days in a row serving meal, after meal, after meal. The gruelling summer heat had been doubly intensified by the kitchen stove raging on full power, struggling to cope with the hordes descending from every corner of the land, wanting to be fed and watered — or so it seemed.

"Why don't we do something next weekend?" Annette made an attempt to buck them up. "Any suggestions?"

"How about a barbecue at my place on Saturday?" Sheila shrugged her shoulders and peered over her cappuccino, her long, brunette fringe mingling with her eyelashes. She lived in a caravan on a derelict farm with her husband, two children and a canary. The latter they had inherited when it flew into the caravan one day having, assumedly, done a bunk from its owner. Her son, Harry, in a flash of inspiration, had decided to call it 'Tweetie' and had become its adopted guardian ever since. Phil, her husband, was converting the farmhouse into a home for themselves, and the adjacent barns were to be transformed into luxury apartments which, if everything went according to plan, would be rented out next year.

"What a brill idea!" Annette became more alert and zoomed into organising mode.

"I can pick you and Joanne up, Carlton, and you could get a taxi home then you can both have a drink. Julian or I could walk back for our car

Sunday morning — if we're in a fit state that is. Perhaps Irene could run the shop with the Saturday staff. You know she doesn't mind covering for us occasionally."

Carlton was nodding solemnly. "It would be quieter next weekend," he was chewing it over, "and his mother liked to help out since her retirement."

It was Irene who had started the business twelve years ago, but she had now passed it on to her son so that she could spend more time with her beloved Raymond.

"It'll probably rain." Carlton, the eternal optimist, was still unconvinced.

"Well, even it it does, we can use one of the barns." Sheila always provided a Plan B.

Luckily, it was a gloriously sunny day. Annette slowly negotiated the narrow dirt track to the farmhouse. Grass, daisies and buttercups were rampant down the middle and the overgrown hedges clipped the sides of the car. A small, brown rabbit darted in front of the bumper, it's bobbed tail scurrying before disappearing into the hedgerow.

"Shame you missed it. We could've had barbied bunny for lunch." Julian cocked his head and winked at Carlton and Joanne in the back.

"Don't be so horrid!" Annette chastised him, but she knew he did not mean it.

Rounding the last bend, the dilapidated farm came into view. Sheila was busy laying the picnic table in the unweeded garden but, as soon as she spotted her guests, she dropped the cutlery and rushed to welcome them, waving as she approached. Amy, her eight-year old, skipped along behind her, blonde curls bouncing in the radiant sunshine.

"Hi! Everyone O.K.?"

"Yes thanks, chooks!" Julian gave her a huge hug before lifting little Amy on to his broad shoulders and trotting off to see what Harry was up to.

"Where's Phil?" Carlton was getting worried there would be no-one to cook his food and there was no way on this earth *he* was slaving over a hot barbecue.

"He's just lit the charcoal and gone to get some burgers out of the freezer."

Sheila heard him breathe a sigh of relief as he bounded in the direction of the booze.

"Another sausage anyone?" Phil was almost on his knees pleading, the few remaining were starting to shrivel.

Annette was bloated to bursting point and groaned. "Sorry, can't eat another thing."

Phil glanced around with his smoke-filled eyes, but heads were shaking vigorously. Disappointed, he slid the juicy sausage off the fork and placed it tidily back on the grill.

"I am so, SO stuffed," Joanne grabbed her waist, convinced it had expanded at least two inches after all she had gobbled down.

Julian, meanwhile, was unfastening the top button on his jeans, exhibiting a white roll of hairy flab which looked as if it hadn't seen the light of day since dinosaurs ruled the earth, but he didn't care two hoots.

"Phil is such a sweetie, you know, Sheila. You're lucky to have him. Not every man would cook for his wife's work mates. Your children are so lovely too." Annette accepted a buttercup from Amy and for a brief moment experienced a flush of envy. Fate had dealt her cruel cards and, despite being truly content with her kind, loveable Julian, she had been unable to bear children of her own. Inch by inch, she scrutinized the farmhouse.

"This place is a bit spooky. Do you know who it belonged to?"

"Well, we think the last farmer was an old eccentric called Mr Evans." Sheila refilled their empty tumblers, the ice cubes clinking against the glass. "We don't know much about him, only that he died in mysterious circumstances. I asked Mr Collins next door, but he clammed up."

The couples gawped at each other, but Annette was curious to know more.

"I bet it's creepy at night." She twiddled a strand of long, auburn hair around her forefinger.

"It is a bit. Sometimes, when I've got up for the loo, I've seen a light flickering in the window above the kitchen."

All of them, catching flies, stared at the broken pane on the first floor.

"Phil and I think it's Mr Evans."

"Have you seen anything, Phil?" Now Joanne was intrigued, her large demure eyes revealing she was hooked.

"No, but I've heard things."

"Like what?" Carlton was sceptical.

"When I've been working late on the house, I've heard footsteps on the ceiling and unearthly moaning and groaning, but I've never had the bottle to go and find out what or who is causing it. Sheila will give you a tour if you like."

A car pulled into the yard, the stones crunching as it reversed and parked next to the caravan.

"Dad!" Sheila strained to push herself out of the plastic chair, weighted down by the mounds she had shovelled, but she was keen to introduce her father to her friends.

"Afternoon all." Sheila's Dad was very jovial. Annette had met him before and loved his bubbly humour and quick wit. He reminded her of a big, excited kid who couldn't wait to blow out the candles on his birthday cake.

"I've been telling them about Mr Evans, Dad. I'm just about to show them round the house."

"Can you eat a sausage?" Phil, eager not to let an opportunity slip, waited for a favourable response, but Sheila's Dad had clocked the burnt offerings and said he had already eaten, muttering 'thank goodness' under his breath.

Sheila led her entourage through the kitchen door, topped up glasses clenched in their hands. There was a freezer, washing machine and little else — apart from Tweetie, of course, swinging merrily on his perch to the raunchy rhythms of Kylie Minogue blaring on the CD player. They meandered into the spacious, square entrance hall where pieces of decayed plaster lay broken on the floor and massive holes exposed the old stone outer shell but, as Sheila shared her vision of log fires crackling in inglenook hearths, their feelings towards the place warmed considerably.

Climbing carefully down the cellar steps, Annette could feel the cold, damp air on her face and the musty smell was nauseating. She hated the dark, had done since she was a child, but she was glad she could not see what was squelching under her feet. She recalled a school trip to a castle torture chamber and the powerful urge to flee from this claustrophobic dungeon became overwhelming.

"I'll see you at the top of the steps." She shivered and clambered upwards, the daylight was beckoning strongly.

Cellar tour over, they sipped their drinks and wandered up to the first floor, avoiding the gaping hole where part of the stairs had collapsed.

"Do you really think it's haunted?" Annette whispered in Joanne's ear.

"I'm keeping an open mind."

"It's all a load of codswallop!" Carlton strutted past them, shaking his head.

Dubiously, they followed Sheila into the bathroom, the infamous room above the kitchen. There was an old-fashioned cast iron bath, covered with a heavy wooden lid, leaning against the wall.

"This is where I've seen the light." Sheila nodded once and intimated with her attractive eyes.

They mooched over to the window and, through the delicate cobwebs, could see the caravan below. Phil was still fiddling with the last of the sausages, wondering what the heck to do with them. Beyond, golden fields of wheat stretched as far as the eye could see, shimmering in the gentle breeze, and the serene landscape helped them to unwind after the stress of the last few days.

Suddenly, the peaceful tranquillity was shattered, as the lid on the bath flew open.

Startled beyond belief, Annette drenched herself in vodka. She froze for a split second as the ghastly body in the bath sat bolt upright and wailed devilishly.

Joanne was glued to the spot, motionless, unable to coax any life into her legs whatsoever, but she managed to muster a feeble squeal whilst Annette, gathering momentum, scarpered towards the door.

Julian and Carlton were ahead of her, jammed together in the doorway, yelling, determined to keep their beers in tact. But their endeavours were all in vain, as she rammed the blocked exit, hurtling the two brave men into the upstairs hallway. There was a frantic tussle for the top of the stairs, but, on hearing the uncontrollable laughter emanating from the bathroom, they stopped nervously in their tracks, beads of sweat glistening on their foreheads.

Sheila, bent double, staggered on the landing, tears streaming down her face. She was closely followed by her Dad clutching the hideous mask of a wrinkled old man in one hand and a grey, spiky wig in the other.

"You … you … you …" Annette huffed, frustrated because she could not think of a word bad enough to hurl at them, now that the penny had dropped.

Carlton pretended he was cool and had twigged, ages ago, that it was all a wind-up. He downed the dregs in his glass and grinned, relieved that the ghoul in the tub was of human origin after all.

Poor Joanne was still cemented to the floor boards, but the abrupt rush of blood to her head was gradually beginning to circulate downwards, revitalising her comatose legs.

"Do you think Phil might have a spare pair of boxers to fit me?" Julian's face was an unusual shade of shocking white, drained, but in a tight corner his humour was paramount.

Into the evening the shindig continued and, as the sun dipped its lower edge behind the horizon, the tipsy merriment quelled. Fatigue and tiredness was settling in.

"It's been a wonderful day, Sheila," Joanne was genuinely grateful, "but, I'm ready for my bed. Do you know the phone number for a taxi?"

"There's one on the blackboard in the kitchen."

Fumbling for her mobile, Joanne glanced automatically at the bathroom window, unconsciously checking there was no light. She swayed and wobbled her way into the semi-darkness and squinted at the numbers chalked on the board. Painstakingly and deliberately, she pressed each number. A floor board creaked upstairs. Coincidence or another trick? She was unsure, but she had heard that name too many times today as the slow, gruff voice answered her call.

"EVANS' Taxis."